Kitty
and
Mr. Kipling

Other books by Lenore and Erik Blegvad

Anna Banana and Me

Rainy Day Kate

A Sound of Leaves

Other books by Lenore Blegvad

Once Upon a Time and Grandma

Other books illustrated by Erik Blegvad

Sea Clocks: The Story of Longitude by Louise Borden

*With One White Wing: Puzzles in
Poems and Pictures* by Elizabeth Spires

Twelve Tales by Hans Christian Andersen

Water Pennies and Other Poems by N. M. Bodecker

(MARGARET K. MCELDERRY BOOKS)

Lenore Blegvad

Kitty and Mr. Kipling

Neighbors in Vermont

Illustrated
by
Erik Blegvad

MARGARET K. McELDERRY BOOKS
NEW YORK   LONDON   TORONTO   SYDNEY

Margaret K. McElderry Books
An imprint of Simon & Schuster Children's Publishing Division
1230 Avenue of the Americas
New York, New York 10020

Book design by Abelardo Martínez
The text for this book is set in Berkeley Book.
The illustrations are rendered in pencil.

Manufactured in the United States of America
2 4 6 8 10 9 7 5 3 1

Library of Congress Cataloging-in-Publication Data
Blegvad, Lenore.
Kitty and Mr. Kipling : neighbors in Vermont / Lenore Blegvad ;
illustrated by Erik Blegvad.—1st ed.
p. cm.
Summary: In 1892, eight-year-old Kitty learns about writing and the world beyond
her Dummerston, Vermont, home when she befriends her new neighbors,
author Rudyard Kipling and his family, who have recently arrived from England.
ISBN-13: 978-0-689-87363-8
ISBN-10: 0-689-87363-8 (hardcover)
1. Kipling, Rudyard, 1865–1936—Juvenile fiction. [1. Kipling, Rudyard, 1865–1936—Fiction.
2. Friendship—Fiction. 3. Authorship—Fiction. 4. Vermont—History—19th century—Fiction.]
I. Blegvad, Erik, ill. II. Title.
PZ7.B618Ki 2005
[Fic]—dc22
2004004143

For Erik Blegvad, Michael Daley, Jessie Haas,
Karen Hesse, Cynthia Stowe, and Nancy Wilson for
their invaluable help and unflagging encouragement
during my work on this book.
—L. B.

Kitty
and
Mr. Kipling

The Jungle Book came today! From dear Mr. Kipling in England, all the way across the ocean to me here in Dummerston, Vermont. And it's two whole books full—with beautiful blue covers and gold pictures on them, and shiny gold edges on all the pages. Inside one book, in Mr. Kipling's own handwriting, it says, "For Kitty, our good Vermont neighbor, from Mowgli and Rudyard Kipling, who miss you most grievously. November 1896."

So at last I have my very own *Jungle Book*! And it begins just as it did when Mr. Kipling first read it to me four years ago, down the hill in Bliss Cottage.

I was only eight years old then, but I still remember every word of it as clear as anything:

"It was seven o'clock of a very warm evening in the Seeonee hills when Father Wolf woke up from his day's rest, scratched himself, yawned, and spread out his paws one after the other to get rid of the sleepy feeling in their tips."

Dear, kind Mr. Kipling. I miss him too though he's only been gone a few months. I don't reckon he's going to come back again, that's why. But now he has sent me Mowgli. And he has sent me India. It's almost like having him here in Vermont again, right here where he wrote *The Jungle Book*.

He says he misses me. But does he really? How could he miss *any* of us after all the things that went wrong for him here?

One long-ago summer, when Kitty was only eight, there was another very warm evening in Dummerston, Vermont. They were all sitting out on the porch after supper, swatting mosquitoes: Mama, Pa, Kitty, and Silas.

Pa's rocking chair creaked as he turned to Mama.

"He's back, did I tell you?" he said. "That English feller who was around here for a few days in February. Came back last night, him and his wife."

"Oh?" Mama said. She slapped calmly at a big mosquito on her arm. "Who was he again?"

Pa looked up at the empty summer evening sky. "Well now," he said, "the wife is old Mrs. Balestier's granddaughter, isn't she? Sister to Beatty Balestier from down our road. Name of Caroline. But that English feller she married, he's called . . . now what's he called, anyway? Got a funny name . . ."

From the peeling porch steps where she and Silas sat, Kitty listened. What with school and the snow and the long boring days to get through, she had forgotten the Englishman who had come to Dummerston briefly that winter. She'd never seen him anyway. But now she waited with interest to hear who he was. Something new in Dummerston? In dull old Dummerston? That would make a change!

But then, *zing!* Kitty jumped up, slapping furiously at her ankle. "There's another one! They're biting me all over the place!"

From the step below, Silas laughed up at her. "Saw that one coming, I did," he said.

"You should have told her," Mama said to him. She waved her hands toward Kitty to chase the flying things away. "That's what a big ten-year-old brother is for."

"Well, now they can bite *him*," Kitty said, coming up the steps, "'cause I'm going in."

Pa paid no attention to them. Then, "Kipling!" he exclaimed. "That's his name. Rud-yard Kip-ling! And you know, I heard tell . . ." he paused and looked up at the sky again ". . . I heard tell he's real famous."

Kitty stopped at the screen door. Famous? She held her breath. And then Mama asked, "Famous? Famous for what?" Just as Kitty would have asked. But Pa didn't much like Kitty asking questions. He said that for an eight-year-old she just plain asked too many. Like how long could she hold her breath before she would die? Why wasn't her hair curly like Mama's? Why didn't woodpeckers hurt their heads when they banged them against trees? Why? Why?

Sometimes Pa or Mama had an answer for her,

but mostly Pa would say, "Now Kitty, you know that's just something else I can't tell you. No point in askin'."

This time, because it was Mama who asked, Pa said, "Don't rightly remember what he's so famous for. We'll know sooner or later. Looks like they'll be around for a while." Turning, he looked straight at Kitty. "Anyways," he added, and she could tell what was coming, another of Pa's sayings, "one thing we *do* know is curiosity killed the cat."

That was why he called her Kitty, even though her name was Mary Sadie.

Mr. Kipling *was* famous. The newspaper Pa brought home from Brattleboro, the big town near them, said so. It was for his writing he was famous. He wrote all kinds of things: stories and verses and books. He wrote a lot about India, where he was born and had worked as a reporter for several years. He wasn't just famous, the paper said: Mr. Kipling was one of the most famous writers in the whole world—and he was only twenty-six years old!

Mama was impressed. "My!" she said. But Kitty was thrilled to her bones. *A famous neighbor!* she said over and over to herself. *I've got a famous neighbor!*

Mr. Rudyard Kipling may have come to live on Kitty's road in Dummerston that summer of 1892, but for a long time almost nobody saw him. He and his wife kept to themselves down there in Bliss Cottage, the tiny house they were renting near to Mrs. Kipling's family. Nobody seemed to mind, though. Nobody but Kitty, that is. She could hardly wait to catch sight of the famous man. Her head was already filled with questions to ask him: about India, about tigers and elephants, about England and if there was a real queen there. If only she could meet him! But she would have to wait—wait and keep her ears open.

The best place for listening was in the general store. Kitty knew you could learn a lot from the gossip there. So she listened. Little by little she learned that Mr. Kipling had met Caroline Balestier, his American wife, in Europe, where one of her brothers, who was a very good friend of Mr. Kipling's, had died.

She learned that the Kiplings had married in England. Now they had come to Vermont to visit Mrs. Kipling's grandmother and younger brother, Beatty, who lived in two big houses down Kitty's road.

But Kitty already knew a few things. Mostly about Mrs. Kipling's brother Beatty. Well, who didn't? Good things and bad: how he drank a terrible lot of whiskey and often got himself into trouble; how he always seemed to get out of it again with a joke and a laugh; how he did wild things like racing his sleigh across the frozen river or driving his team of horses into town—"like a crazy man," as Mama said—making Kitty and the other children jump out of the road when they heard him coming.

But most people liked him anyway. He was an educated man, cheerful when he wasn't drunk or in a temper, generous, and what Mama called "full o' beans." "That's just Beatty," most people said, "doin' and sayin' what he wants."

But Pa said, "Well, folks can call him hearty and such, but me, I call him rowdy."

Of course Silas wanted to be just like Beatty when he grew up.

———◀◇▶———

Pa was a logger. But it was high summer then, which was haying time for everybody, even loggers. On one of those hot days, Pa and Silas and Kitty were riding to the hay field in their wagon. Not far along they came upon a young man they had never seen before standing in the road next to a horse and buggy.

That's him! Kitty said to herself. *That's Mr. Kipling!* He was quite a short man, dressed in old knicker-bockers and a tattered jacket. He was smoking a funny pipe and the sun glittered on the little spectacles he wore above his great big mustache. He sure wasn't a Vermonter.

"Good morning to you, sir, and to you young ones," the man said pleasantly. "Kipling's the name. I'm your new neighbor down below in Bliss Cottage."

Stopping the team, Pa nodded at Mr. Kipling and told him briefly who they were.

Silas poked Kitty hard in the ribs. "Did you hear him?" he whispered, staring at Mr. Kipling. Kitty had heard all right. So that was the way English

people talked, the words all bit off like that! Silas was trying hard not to giggle, but to Kitty, Mr. Kipling's accent had sounded strange and wonderful. She decided right away that all day out in the hay field she would practice saying, "Good morning to you, sir. Kipling's the name."

"I've not been along here before," Mr. Kipling continued, peering up at Pa. "I was just about to take a walk in these beautiful woods. My brother-in-law, Beatty Balestier, tells me you are a logger, so I presume Vermont woods like this are something you know all about."

"Not sure about that," said Pa. "But I know I wouldn't go smoking a pipe in there. Wind's rising and we're mighty short of rain."

That's Pa for you, Kitty thought. Sometimes it could be very embarrassing.

But after that, Pa and Mr. Kipling seemed to get along all right whenever they met on the road or in the town. Logging was what they talked about. Mr. Kipling seemed to want to know everything there was to know about it.

"He's not going to try his hand at logging, is he?" Mama asked one evening before supper.

"I don't guess so," Pa said. "I reckon it's for something he's writing. He's sure got a great curiosity though. Asks a million questions about everything under the sun. Almost as bad as you, Kitty."

Pa chuckled, and to Kitty it seemed like he didn't mind Mr. Kipling's curiosity at all. Why was that? She just had to speak up. "How come he can ask questions and I can't? It's not fair!"

"'Cause you're a little baby, that's why," Silas said with a smirk.

"Silas!" Mama said from the stove where she stood cooking the supper.

Pa didn't even bother to answer. He washed his hands at the sink, combed his hair neatly across the top of his head, and sat down at the table.

"Wash up, you two" was all he said.

"Not fair," Kitty said again, but to herself this time.

During supper, Pa told them he was going down to Bliss Cottage that evening. He had arranged with Beatty to deliver wood there for the Kiplings' cookstove.

When Kitty heard this, she took a deep breath. "Please, Pa," she said in her best-behaved voice, "can I go with you if I'm real good?"

Mama interrupted. "Now, Mary Sadie, you know what we've heard. Mr. and Mrs. Kipling don't like people coming there. They mostly don't even let neighbors in, and none of those newspaper reporters at all, do they? I don't s'pose they'll want you, either."

Kitty knew about the reporters. They were all over the place, even out there on the road by her house, hoping to interview Mr. Kipling for their papers because he was so famous. They came in hired buggies from the train station almost every day. But they just had to turn right around again and go back to Boston or New York. They never even got near him. It was Mrs. Kipling who saw to that. She was very strict. She knew Mr. Kipling hated having reporters chasing after him like they did wherever he went, all over the world. When Kitty saw them passing on the road she wished she could run out and ask them about Mr. Kipling, but she didn't dare.

"Ayuh," Pa said in agreement, "Mama's right about that. What's he call it? 'An invasion of his rights as a citizen' or such like. Wants them to leave him alone. Says they can just call him a boor and be done with it."

"What's a boor?" Silas asked, reaching for a piece of bread and almost knocking over his milk mug.

"It's what you'll grow up to be if you don't mind your manners," Mama said sharply.

"But Mr. Kipling's not a boor, is he?" Kitty asked, questioning again without thinking. She couldn't help herself.

Pa looked sharply at her. "Not so far," he said. "But all these goings-on up here on our hill are something I don't hold with, I'll tell you that."

Then after supper, and after Kitty and Silas had dried the plates and mugs, to Kitty's delight Pa suddenly said, "Now, I've said many a time that he travels fastest who travels alone, but I want to reset those fence rails the colt knocked off this afternoon. Might as well come along, Kitty; you can help me."

Silas watched them drive off. "Look out, Mr. Kipling!" he shouted after them. "Here comes Miss Kitty! She's worse than all them reporters put together!"

"That'll do, Silas," Mama told him.

———◁◦▷———

At Bliss Cottage, Mrs. Kipling made Kitty sit on a chair in the kitchen. She was short like Mr. Kipling, and she "bustled," as Mama would say—she bustled Pa and his wood right out to the woodshed. Kitty sat looking at everything until her eyes nearly fell out of her head. Through a doorway she could see into a little room where a table was set with candlesticks and wine glasses. Hadn't they had supper yet? she wondered. Was it a party? Through another doorway there was a much smaller room. What was in there? Getting up, she tiptoed over to peek in, and to her surprise, there was Mr. Kipling himself, writing at a desk. Mr. Kipling looked up.

"Hello there," he said. "Kitty, isn't it?"

"Yes, sir," Kitty said, backing away. "I'm sorry if I bothered you."

"That's all right." Mr. Kipling smiled. Behind him stood a shelf filled with books covered in leather. Kitty had never seen so many books in her life. She stared at them.

Then, the question bursting out of her, she said, "My pa says you're writing a book about logging. Is that what you're writing there?"

Mr. Kipling laughed. "No, but I might someday."

"Are you writing about India then? About tigers and elephants?" Kitty went on in spite of herself.

Mr. Kipling laughed again and put down his pen. "Well, as a matter of fact, these days I *am* writing about India and about a tiger, as well. How did you guess? And about wolves. But at the moment I'm just writing a rather dull letter."

"Did you ever see one? A tiger, I mean," Kitty asked, wide-eyed.

"Indeed I have," Mr. Kipling replied.

"I've seen four bears," Kitty confided. "There are lots of bears here in Vermont. I'd sure like to see a tiger, though."

"Would you?" said Mr. Kipling. He turned his head to watch Pa and Mrs. Kipling return to the kitchen. "Well, since you're interested, I'd be glad to tell you about them another day if you like. And you can tell me about your bears." He took up his pen again. It was time to go.

"Yes, yes," Mrs. Kipling said, ushering Kitty away and opening the door to let her and Pa out. "Another day."

As the door shut firmly behind them, Kitty heard Mrs. Kipling say a funny thing. "Goodness, Ruddy, look how late it is. There's hardly time to dress for dinner!"

On the way home Kitty thought about that. *She looked dressed to me,* she said to herself.

The next night Kitty just had to ask. "Mama," she said, "am I dressed for dinner?"

"What's that?" Pa said, looking up from his plate. Silas turned to look at Kitty's same old cotton dress.

Mama laughed. "I know what she means," she said. "I heard about it in the store. The Kiplings dress up for dinner in party clothes every night of the week. Better than their Sunday best, even if it's just the two of them. It's what they do over in England. Mrs. Kipling likes that kind of thing, I'm told."

Pa frowned. "Well, it's not England here," he

said. "Not anymore. Hasn't been for over a hundred years. Sounds kinda fancy to me, for Bliss Cottage."

But Kitty thought, *Dressing up for dinner!* How she wished she could see that!

One afternoon, when the day had cooled, Kitty and Mama baked blueberry pies. Silas and Kitty had picked berries in the morning, before the worst of the heat, arguing over every berry, as usual. Now Kitty rolled out the dough with Mama's rolling pin, stopping every so often to make fingerprints into leafy patterns in the leftover scraps.

"Mama, is it true everybody in the world has different fingerprints?" she asked. "Mama, are your fingerprints just like mine? Make me a fingerprint here."

"I haven't time for that," Mama said. "Would you roll out that last piece of dough, please, else we'll never get finished here."

Later, when four pies sat cooling on the kitchen table, Kitty had an idea. "Can we give a pie to Mr. and Mrs. Kipling?" she asked. She held her breath, waiting for Mama's answer.

"That's a neighborly thought," Mama said. "Pa's

going by there later when he goes for some lamp oil. Maybe you can ride with him if he's agreeable to it. But don't be pestering them with your questions, you hear, Mary Sadie? Try to be a good girl."

"Yes, Mama," Kitty said. She would try, she really would, if only she could have a chance to see that famous Mr. Kipling again.

Pa dropped her off at Bliss Cottage. "I'll fetch you in round about half an hour," he said as she climbed down from the wagon. Handing her the pie, he added, "Now don't go pokin' your nose into things that are none of your business."

"No, Pa," Kitty said, but to herself she thought, *A half hour! A whole half hour!* Carrying the pie carefully, she headed past the barn toward the cottage.

"*Pssst, Kitty!*"

Someone was whispering to her from the shadows inside the barn door!

Kitty turned, and there was Mr. Kipling peeking out, a piece of hay caught in his mustache.

"Reporters!" he whispered. "Came right in the side door of the house! I had to make a dash for it."

The barn was dark and smelled of newly stacked hay.

"Are you hiding?" Kitty whispered back.

"I am indeed. Can you imagine it? They came sneaking up on foot from the main road!"

Goodness! Kitty thought. Being famous could be a lot of trouble.

But the blueberry pie made everything better, as Mr. Kipling said as soon as he saw it. And when he had made sure the reporters were gone, he and Kitty each had a piece of it sitting in the house at his writing desk. The Kiplings' new serving maid from Sweden brought it to them. Kitty stared at her with great interest; she had never known anyone who had a serving maid before.

Mrs. Kipling was resting, Mr. Kipling said. That was how the reporters had managed to get so close.

On his desk lay a thick stack of papers. The top sheet was covered with small slanted handwriting.

"Do you want to write about the tiger now?" Kitty asked, remembering her promise to Mama. "I can wait for Pa in the kitchen."

"No, no," Mr. Kipling said, lighting his funny pipe. "I never write after one o'clock. Nine to one,

that's always my writing time. Best time for my demon to take charge as well."

"Your what?" Kitty asked.

"My inspiration. My muse." Kitty must have looked confused, for Mr. Kipling added, "The thing that drives my stories on, you know. Makes my pen write almost by itself. I call it my demon." He took a slip of paper and wrote the word down: *DAEMON*.

That wasn't what Kitty had always thought a demon was. Wasn't it some kind of a devil or something? And was it really spelled like that? But she nodded as if she understood. Moving a bit closer, she looked at the other things on Mr. Kipling's table. A pen in a shiny silver pen holder caught her eye.

"Is that what you write your stories with?" she asked.

"Yes." Mr. Kipling nodded. "Though I'm not terribly fond of it. I used to have a lovely octagonal one made of agate but it broke. Oh, I say . . . this may interest you." He reached for a large pewter ink pot. "See what's scratched in here? The names of all the tales and books I have written with ink from this very pot." There were an awful lot of names, and

22

they certainly were interesting. So were all the other things on his desk: an ink-stained ruler, clips and pins of different sorts, and best of all a paper weight in the shape of a little crocodile.

"Shall I read you a story while we're waiting?" Mr. Kipling asked then, taking the top sheet from the stack of papers. "Well, it's only the idea for a story, really, but it might be something you will like." Pushing his little spectacles high onto his forehead and holding each sheet of paper up close to his eyes the better to see the writing, he began to read. And then, for the first time, Kitty heard the opening words of *The Jungle Book*.

"'It was seven o'clock of a very warm evening in the Seeonee Hills . . .' Rather like it is here this evening, don't you think, Kitty?"

By the time Pa fetched her, Kitty had met Mowgli the man-cub, heard the roar of Shere Khan the tiger, and learned how the wolf pack had accepted Mowgli as one of them in a faraway jungle in India.

Later, riding home with Pa, she couldn't stop thinking about what she had heard. She hardly paid attention to Pa when he said, "Funny thing—I picked up two footsore reporters on the way into town. They sure were hot under the collar. Never got to lay eyes on Mr. Kipling at all. Swore they were going to get back at him one day."

He almost gave a chuckle. Waking up from her daydream, Kitty giggled too. How could she know then that it wasn't anything to giggle about?

Kitty was happy to see that the Kiplings seemed to like living in Vermont. Mr. Kipling said that Bliss Cottage was his first real home. Kitty knew he had traveled to many places all through his life, but he really seemed to feel at home there. People often saw him walking in the woods and the meadows with a book about wildflowers so he could learn their names. And one day after she had gotten to know him a bit better, it was Kitty herself who taught him how to tell evergreen trees apart.

"White pine has five needles," she told him. "Spruce needles are square. Balsams have flat, stiff needles, and their pine cones sit up."

Mr. Kipling was delighted with that and wrote it all down on a piece of paper he had in his pocket.

But he didn't have any Vermont friends except for Beatty, Beatty's wife, and their little daughter, at least not for a long time.

There were *some* people who were allowed to see Mr. Kipling: other writers who came from far away and men who published his books. But no real Vermont friends.

"Well, I'm not surprised," Mama said about that. "I hear tell he wrote some mighty disrespectful things about America a few years back, and even about Vermont folk when he first came here to Dummerston."

"What's *disrespectful* mean?" Kitty asked.

"Criticizing. And making fun of things we do. Like our town suppers and our church sociables. Said we gossip a lot too."

That didn't sound like the Mr. Kipling Kitty knew. But later she found out it was true. He *had* written things like that for English newspapers, and some Vermont and Boston papers had reprinted them when he came to live there.

"Seems like he's got a sharp eye and a sharp tongue both," Mama said.

And later on, just by keeping her ears open, Kitty learned that there were lots of Americans who didn't approve of things Mr. Kipling wrote about or believed in, especially if it was what Pa called "politicking." Pa said it was because Mr. Kipling thought that England was the best of all countries in the world, that America was a wild and dirty place, that England should rule over poorer countries like India and show them how they could improve by behaving like English people, and a lot of other things Kitty didn't understand.

"Imperialism," Pa said it was called. "And us Americans, we don't hold with that."

If Kitty didn't understand much of what "that" was, she guessed many folks in America were suspicious of Mr. Kipling, famous or not. But even so, she heard tell, they kept right on reading anything he wrote, not just in America and England but all over the world in every language under the sun. And wasn't she herself fascinated by everything he said and did?

The Brattleboro paper generously forgave Mr. Kipling. It said he was a genius and that any mistakes he might make were simply "the mistakes of a genius."

Kitty didn't know what a genius was then, but as time passed she realized it meant someone like Mr. Kipling.

Mama didn't let Kitty spend a lot of time at Bliss Cottage that summer.

"If you've finished your chores, there's plenty of other things to do when the weather is fine," she said. "Go and do them."

So without much enthusiasm, Kitty did what she usually did in the summers: She swam in the village swimming hole, she went riding in the meadows, she found a snapping turtle. She and Silas helped Pa paint the barn.

Mr. Kipling was painting too. He and Mrs. Kipling were said to be working extra hard to get Bliss Cottage ready for the winter. People wondered why. Soon Kitty found out the reason.

One afternoon that summer a big storm blew up with sudden strong, high winds. At Kitty's house, hailstones the size of peas clattered on the porch roof, and a little tornado roared across the garden. One of the sugar maple trees split in half and came down with a crash right in Mama's flower beds. After the storm, when Pa needed to clear away the branches, he realized he had left his best ax at Bliss Cottage, so he went to fetch it. When he came back, what a surprise! There was Mr. Kipling riding with him in the buggy.

"I wanted to see with my own eyes that you were all right!" Mr. Kipling exclaimed, jumping to the ground. "Quite an experience!"

Mama assured him they were fine.

"A real little cyclone!" Mr. Kipling went on. "You should see the roads. Almost impassable with fallen branches! Our woodshed roof blew off. And the house, it positively rose a-tiptoe just like a cockerel about to crow!" He seemed delighted with it all.

Mr. Kipling helped to clear away the maple tree branches. It was hot work. Later Mama brought lemonade out to the porch. Mr. Kipling sat with them, rocking in one of the old rocking chairs. It was then they had another surprise.

"You know more about carpentry than I," he said, turning to Pa. "Perhaps you can lend me a hand." He explained that his brother-in-law, Beatty Balestier, who knew a lot about things like carpentry, was too busy to help. He had been put in charge of building a new house for the Kiplings. These days he was laying the foundation, hoping to finish it before winter set in.

Everyone had known for a while now that the Kiplings were probably going to stay in Dummerston and would build a new house if they did. Kitty had been overjoyed when she heard it. But now she saw Mama and Pa exchange glances. She knew what they thought of Beatty Balestier, and that they also understood he needed a steady job to earn money. The Kiplings wanted to help him. But Kitty guessed that Pa and Mama would never have put him in charge of building a house for themselves.

"Some of the old clapboard has blown away at the cottage," Mr. Kipling continued, "just where we're hoping to fix up a cozy little attic room." His eyes were twinkling. "A place to put a new little Kipling, come December."

Oh my goodness! Kitty thought. *A new little Kipling!* How on earth could she wait for that?

———◇———

When the trees began to turn orange and red, it was time to go back to school. Silas and Kitty usually walked both ways, though sometimes Pa took them in the logging wagon.

The year before, Kitty hadn't liked school very much but had not minded going. This year, the school room they were all in together, little kids and big ones, seemed small and crowded to her. The *Vermont Historical Reader* told her things she just couldn't get interested in. What did she care if the production and use of slate in Vermont started in the town of Fair Haven fifty years ago? Her mind was on other things. It was on Mr. and Mrs. Kipling and on life at Bliss Cottage. It was on Mowgli and India. She wanted to know more about them all. Every day she worked hard at getting her chores done quickly after school, because sometimes Mama let her go to Bliss Cottage, where Mr. Kipling was glad to have help getting his house ready for winter. When she was there, she could enter that different world that had been brought by some miracle to dull old Dummerston and to her.

"If it gets as cold as it was when I was here last February," Mr. Kipling said to Kitty one of the days she was at Bliss Cottage, "we'll jolly well have to keep it out of the house, won't we? Thirty degrees below freezing it was! I'll never forget it!"

So Kitty helped pile evergreen branches all around the outside bottom edge of Bliss Cottage to stop the drafts from coming in. She helped stack the firewood that Pa had brought. Mr. Kipling was going to need a lot more of it, she thought. Did he really know how much snow would be coming? Or how very very long the winter would last?

For now, though, there were the autumn leaves in red and gold to astonish him.

"Magnificent!" he exclaimed, looking at the bright trees. "Glorious! It's rather like a battle—no, an insurrection, that's it: an insurrection of the tree people against the waning of the year! That's what I shall call it."

"What's *insurrection*?" Kitty asked a bit hesitantly, not sure yet if Mr. Kipling minded her asking questions.

"It means rebelling, resisting, like your American

Revolution against my country," he replied immediately, looking carefully at her through his little spectacles. "Does that help? Mustn't hesitate to ask, Kitty. Listen, I will tell you a secret. The best servants I ever had I call What and Why and How and Who and Where and When. One day I'm going to write a verse to them. Because without them, I would know nothing at all."

Kitty almost laughed out loud thinking how much Pa wouldn't agree with that. For Pa, curiosity only killed the cat. But Kitty loved coming to Bliss Cottage and hearing the strange things Mr. Kipling said.

And best of all, whenever they stopped working to rest, sitting side by side on a log, Mr. Kipling told her more about Mowgli and India, stories that filled her head to bursting.

The day she forgot to feed the chickens, Mama lost patience.

"Now then, Mary Sadie," she said, "can you remember your chores? You'll be needed to help pick the rest of the apples. Winter's coming, you know."

After that, Kitty could go less often to Bliss Cottage.

But it didn't really matter. By now there were so many of Mr. Kipling's stories inside her head, she had plenty to think about.

Not just about Mowgli and the wolf pack. Mr. Kipling told stories about princesses in blue dresses of silk trimmed with diamonds and rubies; about deadly cobra snakes and tribes of warring monkeys; about palaces with walls of lacy marble, or palm trees that rattled in the wind like dried-out bones. Stories that took her far, far away from the damp cellar where she helped Mama stack the new jars of grape jam on the shelves.

If she was riding with Pa in the wagon hauling bushel baskets of apples, she imagined it was a red lacquered bullock cart decorated with shiny brass peacocks and scarlet curtains. On wet days she thought of the monsoon, the rainy season in India, which the people there would greet with shouts of joy. And how the courtyards in the villages, drenched with rain, would come alive with the croaking of hundreds of frogs.

Oh yes, at last she had plenty of things to think about that were different from Dummerston, Vermont.

———⟨◇⟩———

Kitty didn't know what she was thinking about the day she fell out of the apple tree. She didn't fall far, but she hurt her arm just the same. Mama was worried. She drove Kitty herself to Dr. Conland, their village doctor. Kitty liked Dr. Conland; everyone did. He'd come to see you in the middle of the night, even in the dead of winter, if you needed him. Sometimes he'd tell you exciting tales of his early days as a cod fisherman if you needed cheering up.

Kitty's arm wasn't broken, but Dr. Conland said she had to keep it in a sling for a while. Silas was going to be real jealous, Kitty thought with pleasure as she and Mama started home in the buggy.

But then a strange thing happened. A man came riding down the hill on a bicycle, very fast, his feet up on the handlebars like a schoolboy showing off. Suddenly his bicycle skidded on the bumpy dirt road. The rider lost control, and the machine came rushing straight toward Mama and Kitty! At the very last minute the man managed to swerve, and with a thump he landed himself right in Dr. Conland's full hay cart, which was standing at the side of the road.

"Surely he is dead!" Mama cried out. Both she and Kitty held their breath. But no, whoever it was was moving . . . he was coming slowly out of the hay . . . he was . . .

"Mr. Kipling!" Kitty exclaimed.

"Sorry about that," Mr. Kipling said, climbing out of the hay cart and brushing himself off. He was very pale. "Shouldn't have put my feet up. Rotten idea."

"I should think so," Mama remarked.

Dr. Conland ran out to see what had happened. "A lucky miracle," he called it. But the luckiest thing about it was that right there Mr. Kipling met Dr. Conland, who became his very best friend in Vermont.

When Mama and Kitty told Pa and Silas about Mr. Kipling's accident, everyone laughed. But it was that very same bicycle and another fall that would have a part in the awful things that happened four years later.

The snow came late that winter. Kitty was glad. She hated having to put boots, scarves, and mittens on every time she went out the door. But when the first snow of the year fell, it was exciting anyway. It always was. Thick, silent, and lovely, it quickly made the pine trees on the hills disappear. Soon she couldn't see even as far as the road.

It was a cozy time too. Silas and Kitty worked together on an old jigsaw puzzle without quarreling. Mama stitched her patchwork quilt. Pa just looked happy; logging was much easier on snowy slopes.

Were they doing jigsaw puzzles at Bliss Cottage, too, Kitty wondered, or was Mr. Kipling busy down there in the snow writing about Mowgli's green Indian jungle? How she wished she knew.

Days later, after another snowfall, she had the answer. Pa and Silas and some of the neighbors were out clearing roads with teams of oxen and plowshares chained to logging sleds. As soon as their road was passable, along came Mr. Kipling in his little horse-drawn sleigh, its bells jingling. They were mighty surprised, Mama and Kitty, for Mr. Kipling almost never drove by himself. He wasn't very good at it. A neighbor of his, Miss Cabot, once had to show him how to turn a carriage around in the road, he was so helpless.

But there he was, stomping snow from his boots onto their porch, saying to Kitty, "I rather hoped you couldn't get to school today." He was wearing a fur hat and the longest coonskin coat Kitty had ever seen. She tried hard not to stare. Under one arm he carried a brand new pair of snowshoes, which he held out to her. "I am in the greatest need of instruction in maneuvering these strange things," he announced, "these gigantic lawn-tennis bats! I've been oiling them for days. See, they're ready, are they not? But I simply cannot discover the secret of using them, and I can't wait a minute longer!"

So then and there, out in the fresh snow, Kitty taught Mr. Kipling how to snowshoe.

"You have to keep the heels down!" she shouted at him. "Slide one shoe over on top of the other!"

"But my ankles ache so," Mr. Kipling complained. He was breathless from falling down and picking himself up. Finally he got the idea of it. Then together the two of them went snowshoeing over the deep drifts into the silent woods.

Mr. Kipling was thrilled. "The most beautiful thing I've ever done!" he exclaimed.

Kitty enjoyed snowshoeing too, but for her it was just something ordinary; she had done it all her life. Now she was learning that nothing was just ordinary to Mr. Kipling. He noticed and enjoyed everything there was to see and do.

Christmas came and went, but Kitty hardly paid attention to it that year. She was just waiting for the Kiplings' baby to be born. She did manage to make presents: a big hemstitched handkerchief for Pa, a pinecone picture frame for Mama, and a little birch-bark canoe for Silas. In return she got a beautiful wooden comb, a mirror, and some of her favorite licorice sticks. Pa snowshoed down to Bliss Cottage with spice cookies and cranberry jelly that Kitty had helped Mama make. He came home again with the biggest box of fancy store-bought candy they had ever seen.

The snow was three feet deep by then. The only creatures out in it besides Pa were a flock of wild turkeys, a skinny fox, and a few hares. Every morning the drifts around the house were crisscrossed with their tracks.

But on December 29, someone else was out too. Dr. Conland was driving to Bliss Cottage in that old hooded sleigh of his, because the Kiplings' baby was coming. The baby was coming at last! And when it did, the baby was Josephine.

My, but she was pretty! She had the clearest blue eyes. She had dimples in her chubby cheeks. And she was clever, too, right from the start. Mr. Kipling was delighted with her. Well, more than delighted, Kitty guessed. He always looked at Josephine as if she were too wonderful to be true—or to last.

"Here we are," Kitty heard him say one day, "worshiping a baby in a snow temple!" Mama had let Kitty snowshoe down the hill to see Josephine. Mrs. Kipling was holding the baby in a rocking chair by the window. Outside, the snow glittered in the sun. Mr. Kipling made cooing noises at Josephine as she kicked her feet happily. When one of her tiny woolen booties came off, he tried to put it on her again. "Is there anything so beautiful in the world as a babe's small foot?" he said, gently touching Josephine's tiny toes.

"No," Mrs. Kipling agreed, taking the sock from him and putting it quickly back on Josephine's foot.

"But not if it has frostbite." Mrs. Kipling was a very practical lady. Kitty supposed she had to be; Mr. Kipling wasn't practical at all.

Many things happened after Josephine was born.

There was the nurse from England who came to take care of her. She was called Nanny.

"They've got a nanny goat to take care of their baby," Silas joked. But Kitty was fascinated by Nanny's starched apron and her little white cap.

Then, in the spring, there was the building of Mr. Kipling's new house, with Beatty Balestier in charge of the workmen.

There was Mr. Kipling's father, come all the way from India to visit for many months. Everyone liked him. He was an artist and could draw pictures of anything under the sun. Whenever Kitty saw him, she asked for a picture of Mowgli or Bagheera, the black panther, to put on the wall of her room.

Finally, in the summer, there was the Kiplings' move to their new house.

In and among all these changes, there were trips Mr. Kipling took, to New York or to Canada. Kitty just couldn't help pestering Pa. "Is he back yet? Is he leaving again? Where's he going *now*?"

Pa knew the answers, for once in a while he helped out on the house if Beatty could use him. But all he said to her was, "You'd do well to remember what killed the cat, Kitty."

Well, Kitty was busy during those months too. She and Silas had school. They helped Pa cut ice blocks from the pond for the ice house. They went sliding on their sleds. And at the end of winter, when maple sugaring time came, they helped gather the sap. Kitty liked doing that unless the snow was still too deep. Then it was hard work.

Sugaring time meant spring was coming. And spring meant mud season. But then came daffodils and open windows and robin redbreasts. Soon it was planting time again, and apple blossom and lilac time. The black flies came back too, and so did the grippe. Silas got it that year. Kitty got whooping cough instead and couldn't go to Bliss Cottage for weeks.

So the seasons changed just like always. Baby Josephine changed too. She grew bigger and prettier. Then finally Kitty had her first visit to the new house.

It stood high up on a sloping piece of land near Bliss Cottage, across the road from Beatty's house. The Kiplings had bought the land from Beatty.

The new house had a strange name. It was called Naulakha. It was a big house, a very big house.

"Nau . . . lak . . . ha," Kitty said to Mr. Kipling one day, sounding it out. "Why does it have such a funny name?"

They were sitting with Josephine on one of the new porches. Mr. Kipling called them verandas. There was a view past Mt. Wantastiquet, on the other side of the river valley, all the way to Mt. Monadnock in New Hampshire. Even the view was big. The new house didn't look like a regular Vermont house at all. Mr. Kipling called it a ship, and it *was* like one: a huge, forest-green wooden ship and Kitty wasn't sure she liked it at all.

"It's not as funny a name as Wantastiquet, I'm bound to say," Mr. Kipling replied, jiggling Josephine on his knee. "It's from India. In Hindi it means 'precious jewel.'"

Kitty liked that. Whenever houses in Vermont had names, they weren't very interesting. Mountain Farm or Maplewood, like Beatty's house. But "precious jewel"—Naulakha—that was something different!

Inside Naulakha it was different too, but here as well, Kitty wasn't sure she liked it. There was furniture carved out of a wood called teak. There were brass-topped tables that stood on fringed rugs with strange patterns, and most of the rooms had polished wooden walls and cupboards. She thought it looked bare, not like a cozy Vermont farm house at all. But it did have something remarkable: a wall that could be raised up to make an open porch out of the living room! Mr. Kipling called this the loggia.

Mr. Kipling loved Naulakha, but Kitty wasn't sure what Mrs. Kipling thought of it. She heard that Mrs. Kipling had told someone it was too far from town for her to get the things she needed. But Mr. Kipling loved everything about it: how much room it had after Bliss Cottage, its many closets, the big white bathtub with the oak wood edge, the servants' rooms, the loggia, and the verandas. There was even a playroom on the top floor with a billiard table. But Mr. Kipling was proudest of his study

with its many bookshelves, its fireplace, and its mountain views. If he wasn't helping Beatty work on the house whenever he could be of use, he sat there every morning from nine to one, writing his many verses and stories and letters. From her office in the next room, Mrs. Kipling kept guard and made sure he wasn't interrupted by anyone, ever.

When Kitty was at Naulakha it was always like going on an adventure. Though the Kiplings were almost like a real Vermont family by then, they and their big house were still mysterious and strange to her. How wonderfully different Dummerston had become!

———◁◦▷———

"What's that supposed to be?" Silas said to Kitty one evening. She was at the table sewing something made of scraps of colored cloth.

"Nothing," she replied, not bothering with him.

Silas could see perfectly well what it was. It was a little rag doll complete with cotton dress and cross-stitched blue eyes.

"Funny-looking doll," he commented. Pa looked up from the Brattleboro paper.

"Looks all right to me," he remarked.

Pa knew Kitty was making the doll for Josephine. He would be driving her down to Naulakha the next day to deliver it. Pa worked often at Naulakha these days, and during that time he seemed to have come to like Beatty better.

"I reckon he's just a plain-speakin' Vermonter," Pa would say about Beatty. "Doin' what he wants, sayin' what he thinks."

But he didn't hold the slightest bit with Beatty's drinking, his bad language, or his wild ways.

Neither did Mr. and Mrs. Kipling, especially not Mrs. Kipling, who always seemed to be annoyed with her brother for one reason or another.

The next day Kitty took her rag doll to Josephine. She had never made a doll before, and sewing came hard to her. It hadn't turned out just as she had wanted, but she was proud of its little gingham dress. Josephine was delighted with it. She clutched it tightly, stared seriously into its eyes, and hugged it over and over.

They were sitting on one of the verandas with Nanny when suddenly Mrs. Kipling's voice could be heard clearly from inside the house.

"Mercy's sake, Rudd! Why can't he grow up! He's always, always been like that, Beatty has, even when we were children!" The voice was irritable. "He's got a wife and daughter now. Why can't he behave better, if only for their sakes?"

Mr. Kipling's reply was just a low murmur. But Kitty thought it sounded sad.

At home she pondered over it. Finally, at supper, she just had to ask.

"Pa, why is Mrs. Kipling so angry with Beatty?"

Mama clicked her tongue at her to say it wasn't any of her business. Pa put down his knife and fork, looking serious.

"Money," he said. "That's what it is. Beatty is real careless with it. And being careless with money means trouble. 'Specially if it's not yours." He frowned at Kitty and Silas. "Like I tell you, a fool and his money are soon parted. You hear, you two?"

"Yes, Pa," they said, and waited for more. But that was all.

So once again curiosity meant Kitty had to keep her ears open. But when she finally did learn more, she was sorry; it wasn't part of the adventure at all.

Pa was right. Beatty was careless with money: careless paying the builders Mrs. Kipling had given him the money for; careless with his own money, spending it on drink or just plain giving it away to friends—generously, but carelessly too.

It was Mrs. Kipling's job to take care of the money for Naulakha. She and Beatty argued over it constantly. She only paid him a little at a time so he wouldn't misuse it. That turned him real ornery.

"You're an uppity woman!" he would shout at her so everyone could hear. "Treating me like a little boy. You've got no right!"

And Mr. Kipling was sad, because he really did like his brother-in-law, Beatty, just as most people did. But he had to take Mrs. Kipling's side.

Kitty could tell something was going very wrong. It was like a splinter she'd once had in her finger that didn't bother her much at first but later on turned into real trouble.

There was much gossip in the store about Beatty and the Kiplings. Everyone knew about the arguments, because Beatty complained loudly in the bar of the Brooks House Hotel in Brattleboro to anyone who would listen.

And folks *did* listen, for no one ever really knew what to make of "the Balestier girl" and that writer from England she had married.

They didn't know what to make of Naulakha, either. Wasn't Mr. Kipling poor when he lived in tiny Bliss Cottage? Just look at the worn-out, weather-beaten clothes he always wore. Well, now they knew better. Even Silas began to see what a really famous man he must be.

"Gosh, Mr. Kipling must be rich!" he said. "That house is bigger than the town hall!"

Then there was the well at Naulakha. Sometimes Kitty went with Pa to watch it being dug. It took so long that folks made bets on how deep it would go before they found a good enough flow of water.

"Three hundred and fifty feet! Well, I never!" said Mama when it was finished. "That must have cost a heap!"

After that came new horses, carriages, and sleighs. A stable, a coach house, and a driveway. And later on a rose garden outside Mr. Kipling's study. Yes, people did talk.

"And he makes all that money out of a ten-cent bottle of ink!" they marveled.

Mr. Kipling didn't pay much mind to what people said. He seemed happy having a real home of his own at last. He loved Naulakha and loved working on it whenever he could be of help. There was still lots to be done, summer and winter.

One bitter-cold winter evening Pa said at supper, "They're going to try again to put up Mr. Kipling's windmill tomorrow. I hear Beatty's asking for extra hands." Mr. Kipling needed the windmill to pump water from his new well, but putting it up wasn't an easy job.

Kitty begged to go along, and the next morning she rode down to Naulakha with Pa. Mrs. Kipling let her watch, together with Josephine, from inside the house.

Two yokes of oxen and nine red-faced men slipped and slid on the icy ground. Pa, Beatty, and Mr. Kipling himself pulled and pulled on the frozen ropes. At last the windmill was up, even if it was a bit crooked.

Afterward, when Pa stood talking to some of the men, Mr. Kipling came stomping into the house in his snowy boots. He took off his enormous fur coat and hat, his gloves and scarves, and he piled them any which way into the closet by the front door. Kitty could tell he was "out of sorts," as Mama often said about Silas.

"Well," Mr. Kipling exclaimed when he saw Kitty. "Your Vermont winters aren't just jingling sleigh bells and pretty snowflakes, are they now, Miss Kitty? No sir!" He threw himself into a chair by the fireplace as Mrs. Kipling took Josephine off to make tea.

Kitty wanted to ask when the windmill would begin pumping water. Then she thought better of it. Somehow, she didn't want to hear what else Mr. Kipling might say about Vermont. She just wanted him to go on liking everything. Tiptoeing out, she went to find Pa for the ride home.

There were parties at Naulakha that Christmas, Mr. Kipling's second in Vermont. One was a party for Brattleboro school children. Silas and Kitty were invited too. During the party Mr. Kipling delighted everybody by reciting long verses he made up as he went along, tapping out the rhythms on a tabletop.

Next to Kitty one of the teachers who was there began to write down some of Mr. Kipling's verses. Quick as a fox, Mrs. Kipling came across the room to stop her.

"I'm afraid I can't permit that," she said in a firm voice. The teacher blushed in embarrassment. Well, she didn't know what Kitty knew, that Mrs. Kipling protected everything Mr. Kipling ever wrote or said. It was all very valuable, every word. His signature especially was worth a great deal of money. People wrote asking for it every day from all over the world but without much luck. Being famous was very strange, Kitty told herself.

When the Christmas party was over, Kitty stayed on a little while. Mrs. Kipling had asked Pa to take some of the schoolchildren home in his sleigh. While she waited for him, Kitty and Mr. Kipling played a kind of hide-and-seek with Josephine in his study. "Peep-o game," he called it. It was played hiding behind his big chair. Josephine was walking by then and into everything. Mr. Kipling thought whatever she did was wonderful.

"Look at that!" he exclaimed when she pulled the leather-bound books from his shelves. "She'll be reading before we know it. What's she chosen this time? Ah, Dickens. Splendid choice, Miss Kipling. My compliments." Swinging her into his arms, he hugged her to him. Josephine giggled and buried her head in his tweed jacket.

Kitty watched them, thinking of her own Pa. Had he ever played that way with her? she wondered.

She couldn't remember, but she was pretty sure he hadn't. It just wasn't his way.

"Look at Kitty," Mr. Kipling said to Josephine. "She's stopped frivoling. What shall we do to make Kitty frivol again?" Josephine stopped laughing and put on a long face, copying Kitty's. It made Kitty laugh to see her. "That's better," Mr. Kipling said. "Mustn't be too serious, you know. Must never stop being a child. Have to frivol, especially if you're a parent, or your children won't listen to you for a minute."

Kitty thought Mr. Kipling knew how to "frivol" very well, whatever the word really meant. But she guessed that Mrs. Kipling wasn't very good at it.

"Did your Mama and Papa frivol when you were a little boy?" she asked Mr. Kipling.

"Ah," said Mr. Kipling, suddenly looking serious himself now. "When I was a little boy I was in a place where no one frivoled at all. My sister and I had been sent to England. Our parents were far away in India. We lived with a family who disapproved of everything I did and punished me accordingly." He frowned, remembering.

"Were you bad?" Kitty asked. She tried to imagine Mr. Kipling as bad as Silas but she couldn't.

"Yes, I rather think I was. And I got beaten for it too, which I probably deserved. But worse than beating, do you know what they did? They took my books away. I suppose I liked reading too much and making up stories in my head. It was not approved of." Mr. Kipling told her this in a low voice, maybe talking more to himself than to her. Behind him his many shelves of beautiful books glowed in the firelight. Kitty looked at them with new interest. For Mr. Kipling, having his books taken away had been worse than being beaten.

"I learned to tell lies there," Mr. Kipling continued, "just to stay out of trouble. My start as a writer of tales, you might say. Do you know, they put a sign on my back: 'Kipling, the Liar.'" He stared into the fire, stroking Josephine's hair.

"That doesn't sound like a very nice place," Kitty said in a shaky voice.

"I call it the House of Desolation," Mr. Kipling said. "Do you know what *desolation* means?" Kitty shook her head.

"Misery," he explained. "Loneliness. We were

there for six long years, my sister and I." Then, looking down at Josephine, he suddenly tickled her in the ribs. "But you, my dear Miss Kipling, are never going to know anything like that, are you? Are you?" Josephine exploded into giggles and Kitty giggled with her, relieved to change the subject.

Just then Pa knocked on the door and came in. He smiled to see them. "Time we got home, Kitty," he said.

Kitty jumped up and took hold of his hand. No, Pa didn't frivol and probably never had. But it didn't matter at all.

Mr. Kipling walked them to the door, carrying Josephine. "Thank you for your help," he said to Pa. "It made the party even more enjoyable. A perfect party, I should say. And the end to another perfect year!"

Another perfect year, Mr. Kipling had said, but to Kitty it seemed just then that things began to go wrong. Did it start with Mrs. Kipling getting more and more upset with her brother, Beatty, as time went on? Kitty wasn't sure when it began. She knew something was happening, because at home Pa told Mama about things he had heard at Naulakha, and

Kitty overheard Mama giving her opinions. Mama's voice carried because their walls were so thin.

"Dear me," Kitty overheard Mama say once, "it must be hard on the Kiplings. I've heard tell they promised the brother who died over there in Europe that they would take care of Beatty. And him bein' so difficult to look after. Dear me."

"Stubborn as mules, both of them," Kitty heard her say another time about Mrs. Kipling and Beatty. "Well, like brother, like sister. But it can't be easy for him havin' to come to her for every penny, can it?" That made Kitty think: like Silas, like Kitty? She hoped it wasn't true.

But if she counted them up, not all things were going wrong in those years. There was still much that was fascinating and exciting.

There was the time Mr. Kipling came to Kitty's house one winter evening, driven there by his coachman. He sat with the family around the table in the light of the smoking oil lamp. Of course Silas had forgotten to trim the wick that morning to keep it from smoking, which was one of his chores. Kitty was doing her schoolwork. Silas was whittling a piece of wood, trying not to cut himself.

Mr. Kipling took a sheet of paper out of his pocket. "I've come to ask your opinion on a project of mine," he said, turning to Pa. "You may have heard that I receive rather a lot of post."

Kitty knew "a lot of post" meant he got a lot of mail. But Silas wrinkled his nose in confusion.

"Hundreds of letters a day by now," Mr. Kipling continued. That was a surprise. Kitty knew he picked up his mail in Brattleboro every day, in all kinds of weather, but *hundreds* of letters? "So I've come up with a plan," Mr. Kipling went on. "I'm going to ask the government for a new post office, near here, right down close to the main road. It would be a tremendous help to me, as you may imagine. But I'm told I need all my neighbors to agree. Quite correct. Must obey the law, you know. Now, how would you feel about such a thing?"

"Where you thinkin' of puttin' it?" Pa asked calmly, as though it were the most ordinary thing in the world.

"It appears Mr. Waites' farm has got room," Mr. Kipling said.

Kitty just had to interrupt. "You can't just ask

and get your own post office, can you?" she said in amazement. "Can anyone do that?"

"Hush up, Mary Sadie," Mama said.

But Mr. Kipling smiled. "I think if you were to receive hundreds of letters a day, Kitty, you should be able to as well as I. Why not?"

It took more than a year, but with the help of some of his friends who knew very important people— even President Grover Cleveland—Mr. Kipling got his post office! Being famous wasn't all bad, Kitty had to decide that time.

No, not everything was going wrong then, but so many things were happening, both good and bad, Kitty could hardly keep track. She decided one day to write them down. Taking a pencil from her school satchel and tearing a page from her copybook, she sat down on the edge of her bed to write. Wishing she had a table with stacks of paper like Mr. Kipling's in her room, she made a list:

Things I Remember, 1894–1895
1. Mr. Kipling finished all the stories in what he

calls *The Jungle Book*. There are so many, he says they will fill up two whole books! He says he knew when he was finished writing them because his "demon," or "daemon"—that thing that tells his pen what to write—turned itself off just like a faucet! He has promised to give me a very special copy of them.

2. The Kiplings traveled an awful lot. They went to Bermuda and England and New York and Washington D.C. our capital and Cape Cod. But Mr. Kipling says that when he is away he misses Vermont. What Mr. Kipling misses: fireflies, katydids, fizzy soda water, and me! I miss him too when he is away.

3. Mr. Kipling hired a new coachman from England. His name is Matthew Howard. He wears a top hat and shiny boots and a fancy coachman's uniform every single day! People thought he was a snob at first, like Mrs. Kipling, but he's real nice. It's funny to see him driving on our dirt roads and through the woods all dressed up like

in the circus. When he came, it made Beatty even angrier than before because he takes care of jobs Beatty is supposed to do at Naulakha but doesn't.

4. Beatty gets drunk a lot, and awful ornery. Once he crashed his wagon right into the side of his own barn in a terrible temper when he had too much to drink.

5. Pa says Beatty is always in trouble over money and the house accounts at Naulakha. He owes money to lots of people too. Mr. and Mrs. Kipling are very very upset. I worry that they will stop liking Vermont and move away.

6. The windmill had to come down. It was squeaky and didn't work right. Mr. Kipling was funny—he called it the "Unnecessary Pillywinkle." They got a pump instead, and now Naulakha always has water even in a drought because their well is dug so deep. Ours runs dry a lot.

7. Here's the best thing on my list: a new Kipling will be born early in 1896!

But Kitty's list was incomplete. She didn't write down the many things that had happened that she couldn't understand.

One of those things happened on the Fourth of July, after the town parade. On that day, every summer, Silas and Kitty helped Mama make ice cream. Making ice cream was hard work. Ice from the ice house had to be crushed into little chips and put in the outside part of the freezer tub with the salt. Then the crank handle had to be turned and turned until the cream and the berries and the custard inside the tub froze. Every year when it got to the turning part, Silas lost interest.

"Aw, it's too hot today," he said that year, in the summer of '95. "I'm goin' fishin'." It *was* hot. Kitty was hot too, but she knew how good that ice cream was going to taste. Besides, Silas had just gone fishing the day before with his friends.

"If you don't help, you don't get ice cream," Kitty said crossly, struggling with the crank handle.

"Well, it's too hot," Silas repeated. "Why do we have to make ice cream every Fourth of July?

What's so great about the Fourth of July anyway?"

"You're mighty patriotic, you are," Kitty puffed angrily at him. *Patriotic* was a word Pa liked to use.

"Ha!" Silas snapped back. "You're not so patriotic yourself, Miss Kitty. You're a mighty good friend of someone who doesn't like us Americans much. And you always think he's so perfect, your Mr. Kipling, don't you? Well, why don't you ask him about Veneza . . . Vene . . . Venezuela. Go on, ask him, and see how patriotic *you* are bein' his friend!" Silas looked pleased with himself, saying all this.

Kitty stared at him. What was he talking about? What was Venezuela? What did it have to do with Mr. Kipling, who was in England for the summer anyway?

She discovered later that it was the boys Silas went fishing with who put all those ideas into his head. He wouldn't have known it by himself. They had heard tell that Mr. Kipling was writing angry things against America, which was in a disagreement with England over something happening in Venezuela, a country somewhere in South America. Kitty didn't understand one word of it. But nevertheless, it was part of what went wrong for Mr. Kipling there in Vermont.

One day at the end of that summer after the Kiplings had come back from England, Kitty was at Naulakha. She was helping Mr. Kipling pick out spring bulbs from a garden catalog. They were out on the upstairs veranda with Josephine and Nanny.

Suddenly Mr. Kipling closed the catalog and put it on the footstool next to him.

"Not much point in this, really," he said, looking out across the valley to Mt. Wantastiquet.

"Aren't you going to plant any more daffodils?" Kitty asked.

"No more daffydils?" echoed Josephine.

"We'll see," Mr. Kipling said. "Don't know what I'm going to do yet. Depends on your president, actually." And with that he got up and went into the house.

Goodness, Kitty thought. *What is he talking about?* So of course she had to ask Pa at supper. To her surprise, Pa gave her an answer, and it was longer than usual.

"He's worried, that's what," Pa said. "He thinks there could be war between England and us Americans over this Venezuelan thing. Something to do with borders down there in South America."

War! Kitty said to herself. That sounded terrible!

"You reckon he's right?" asked Mama, holding her fork full of baked beans in midair.

"Nope," Pa said, "I don't. But if you were Mr. Kipling now, thinkin' about a war, you'd maybe plan to get away from America before it happened, wouldn't you? 'Cause this here'd be enemy country for an Englishman and his family, wouldn't it? That's what's on his mind, I reckon: war. Pass the beans, Silas."

At last Kitty understood. If Mr. Kipling wasn't going to be here in the spring to see the daffodils bloom, why should he plant any more of them?

Pa was right. There was no war. The disagreement was eventually settled peacefully. But they didn't know that then. So during the winter Naulakha was a gloomy place. Mr. Kipling's worries and Mrs. Kipling's arguments with Beatty all brought a kind of dark cloud over the whole hill. It was rare now for a trip to Naulakha to feel like an adventure.

Yet once in a while it still was. Like the winter afternoon when Mama sent Kitty to Naulakha on snowshoes.

"You can take a jar of applesauce and some cornbread down to Mrs. Kipling," Mama said. "She'll not be feeling too well with the new baby coming soon. Mind you're back before dark, Mary Sadie. Don't linger."

So Kitty went, but not as happily as usual. First she delivered the presents to Mrs. Kipling, who seemed pleased enough with them. Then she played tea party with Josephine. Josephine had a doll's china tea set all her own and loved pouring make-believe tea into the little cups.

When Kitty finally left, she saw Mr. Kipling outside in the snow, teaching Reverend Day, another good friend he had made in Vermont, how to play a new game called golf. Kitty was sure it was supposed to be played on grass in the summertime. But there was Mr. Kipling playing it out in the snow.

"Hello there, Kitty!" Mr. Kipling called to her.

"Want to try a spot of snow-golf? You just have to hit the ball into one of those tin cans over there in the snow, and you win! Nothing to it. I've inked all the golf balls red so you can see them better."

Kitty hesitated. It looked like fun, with the inked balls leaving wobbly pink tracks in the snow. But it was getting late. She waved good-bye and started for home. On the way she thought to herself that Mr. Kipling had looked happy that afternoon, almost the way he used to. He hadn't looked that happy in several weeks, not since the strange news had come that two railway stations out in Michigan had been named after him—one called Rudyard and one called Kipling.

"Think of it, Kitty," he had laughed when he told her. "We have two railway stations in the family now! The Michigan twins!" He had picked up Josephine and trotted around the room with her. "All aboard for Rudyard!" he had sung out. "All aboard for Kipling and points north!" And Josephine had laughed with him. A bright moment among clouds.

——◇——

"Can we have a new garden?" Kitty said to Mama one day. "Mrs. Kipling's going to make one in their meadow. She's been picking out plants from a catalog." It seemed like Mr. Kipling hadn't wanted to worry Mrs. Kipling about not planting flowers if a war was coming.

"What on earth do I want another garden for?" Mama exclaimed. "Those we have are enough work as it is."

"But I mean a pretty one with only flowers and little paths." Kitty had seen Mrs. Kipling's plans.

"Nonsense," Mama said.

"Which meadow's it goin' in?" Pa asked, interested. When Kitty told him he rubbed his hand across his mouth thoughtfully. "Now that'll make trouble," he said. "Back when they bought their land from Beatty, Mrs. Kipling promised him he could always mow that meadow to feed his animals."

And sure enough, the plan for the new garden put Beatty in a terrible temper. "And he's probably not even needin' the hay," Pa commented, but that didn't matter. By then Beatty and his sister were fighting over everything. This time he swore he would never talk to her again, and for months he didn't.

Now, whenever Kitty passed Naulakha or Beatty's house, Maplewood, she felt very sad. She was sure Mr. Kipling felt that way too and that he really liked Beatty. They had all gotten along so well in the beginning. How could everything have changed so fast?

At school her teacher called her melancholic. "Mary Sadie," the teacher would say, "you're looking mighty melancholic today." And Kitty, upon learning it meant sad and depressed, had to agree— she was very melancholic indeed.

One day Pa said to Mama, "Looks like Naulakha's fancy water pump has broken down. They're havin' to fetch water from Beatty's well, and them not even speakin'. It's a fine howdy-do for neighbors to be in." But now there were no questions from Kitty. She didn't want to know anything about it at all. Something had happened to her curiosity. Whatever she heard about Naulakha now made her as fearful as she used to be of the dark when she was very little.

But she wasn't little anymore. It was 1895, and

she was eleven years old. Josephine was three and could play games and listen to the stories Mr. Kipling loved to tell her. Silas at thirteen was as bad as ever. And Mowgli, at the end of *The Jungle Book,* was seventeen! After many brave deeds he had gone back to his own people exactly as Akela, the wise old wolf, had always said he would.

They were all growing up, but Kitty no longer felt brave or sure about anything. She was not like Mowgli at all.

So the winter was a cheerless one, though the sun shone almost every day and sparkled the snow into diamonds. It was cheerless even though skidding logs down the icy hills was so much easier for Pa that he finally promised to make Kitty a table for her room. And it was cheerless even though Silas slipped at the edge of the ice pond and had to run home with his clothes almost frozen stiff.

The Kiplings and Beatty still weren't talking. Mr. Kipling became even more worried about war because of the new baby that was coming. But nevertheless, early in February of the new year, there was a happy time for a while when Josephine's baby sister, Elsie, was born.

One day Kitty went down to Naulakha to bring Baby Elsie a tiny sweater Mama had knitted for her. It had pretty pink silk ties that Kitty herself had sewn on.

Josephine greeted her gaily. "Tum and see my baby! Tum and see!"

Kitty followed her up to the nursery. At the top of the stairs they met Mr. Kipling coming down.

"Ah, Kitty," he said. "I see you've heard about our new she-child. Have a look at her and come tell me what you think before you leave, all right?"

So later on, in Mr. Kipling's study, Kitty said, "She's real pretty, Baby Elsie. And guess what—Nanny even let me hold her!"

"Did she now?" Mr. Kipling said. "At that rate you'll make a good nanny yourself one of these days." He turned in his chair to look closely at her. "But I dare say you've got other plans for your future, haven't you, Kitty?"

Plans for her future? How could she answer a question like that, out of the blue?

"No," she said, blushing. "I don't have any . . . any plans. Just to get finished with school, I guess."

Mr. Kipling looked serious. "You know, Kitty," he said, "you mustn't 'just get finished' with anything. You must be proud of whatever you do or decide to do: farming, building a house, writing a story, teaching school perhaps. Whatever you do you must do it proudly." He waved a hand in the air. "And take great interest in it! To be doing, to be working, to be a person of action, that's what tells us who we are in the universe."

It is? Kitty said to herself. Again she didn't understand exactly what Mr. Kipling meant. But later on, when she thought about it, it reminded her a little of one of Pa's sayings: "The world is your cow, but it's you who has to do the milkin'."

Sometimes a single word can be frightening. Kitty heard one at school, said by a big boy to his friend. The word was "bankrupt."

"Who'd you say?" the friend asked. "Beatty Balestier?"

The answer was lost in the March wind as the boys barreled out the door on their way home.

It was mud season, and the wind that day was stinging. Kitty ran home through it all without noticing. Bankrupt, they had said. Bankrupt and Beatty. What did it all mean?

"It could mean Beatty's runnin' out of money," Mama told her. "I don't s'pose it's come to that, though. Those boys are just nasty gossips."

"But what does it mean, *bankrupt*?" Kitty insisted.

"It means when there's no more money," Mama said. "When someone can't pay his bills and such. And it means people can have something to gossip about, too. But," Mama added, "he *is* bad with money, Beatty is."

"But what will happen to him?" Kitty asked.

"I don't know," Mama said, a bit impatiently. "But I do know what Pa would be tellin' you right now if he was here."

"So do I,'" Kitty said glumly. "'Say nothin' and saw wood,' I reckon."

"Something like that," Mama said, smiling a little.

———◇———

In spite of Baby Elsie's arrival, a dismal veil still lay over the hill. Anxiously, Kitty waited to see what would happen. What *did* happen was only more trouble.

Soon it was learned around town that Mr. and Mrs. Kipling had thought of a plan to help Beatty out. They would pay his debts if he would stop drinking, go away, and find a steady job. He was not to return home until he could support his wife and daughter properly, and while he was away, the Kiplings would take care of them.

This offer made Beatty so furious that Kitty and her family could almost hear his answer all the way up at their house.

Kitty could hear quite clearly what Mama and Pa were saying downstairs some evenings when they thought she was asleep.

It was a few weeks later she heard Pa say, "Mr. Kipling now, down at Brooks House Hotel, he's been talkin' about Beatty to some nosy person. Seems he said he's had to carry Beatty by the seat of his britches for quite a while." Pa had used those same words to Silas once, Kitty remembered: "If you're wantin' money in your pockets, Silas, you'll have to work for it. Don't go expectin' me to carry you by the seat of your britches."

Now Mama's voice was saying, "I thought all Mr. Kipling talked about these days was cod fishin'." Her voice was joking. Everyone knew that Mr. Kipling, helped by Dr. Conland, was learning all about cod fishermen in Gloucester, Massachusetts, for a new book.

"Well, he should have stuck to fish," Pa said, but his voice wasn't joking. "Talkin' about Beatty's not a good idea in places where Beatty's got friends to tell him things. Means trouble."

Up in her warm bed, Kitty felt a sudden chill, a winter icicle of fear slipping along her spine. Quickly she put her fingers in her ears.

Silas was one of the first to know what happened next. One afternoon early in May, when the Kiplings and Beatty still weren't talking, Silas and his friends were playing tag among the big pine trees below Naulakha. All at once they heard the sound of bicycle tires skidding out on the dirt road, and the thump of someone falling with a cry. They heard a wagon and a team of horses come clattering wildly down the hill. They heard shouting. It was Beatty, roaring like a bull, "See here! I want to talk with you!" They heard Mr. Kipling's voice reply sharply, "If you have anything to say, say it to my lawyers!"

From behind the trees Silas and his friends watched Mr. Kipling pick up his bicycle. They saw blood on Mr. Kipling's hand. They heard Beatty, red-faced and wild with anger, order Mr. Kipling to take back lies he had been telling people about him in the Brooks House Hotel. And they couldn't miss the terrible language Beatty used: "Liar! Cheat! Coward!" And other words Silas was not even allowed to think about.

Frightened, the boys ran off. Later Silas was never quite sure whether he had heard what all the papers said had come afterward. It was reported that Beatty had threatened to kill Mr. Kipling unless, within one week, he took back the things he had been saying about Beatty!

At home, telling about all this, Silas was pleased with himself. Mama and Pa listened in shocked silence. But Kitty listened in absolute horror. She

wished she could run to Naulakha to see how badly Mr. Kipling was hurt, but she knew she couldn't. And she knew also that worse things would be coming soon.

Mr. Kipling was terribly upset. Mrs. Kipling was terribly angry. He was so upset and she was so angry that in a rush that same day they decided to place a charge against Beatty with the town sheriff. And in a day or so, to Beatty's great surprise, and though he had told someone he was sorry for what had happened, Beatty Balestier was arrested.

That evening Kitty complained sadly to Mama as she helped prepare supper. "I can't even go to Naulakha anymore," she said. "I saw Matt Howard in the driveway there and he said Mr. Kipling won't see anybody at all, he's feeling so poorly."

"Oh dear," Mama said with a sigh. "If only they had just let it all cool down. I bet it was *her* idea goin' to the sheriff right off, like that. Always been hard on that brother of hers. Well, I can just imagine what will happen now."

Kitty turned away. She busied herself at the

sink, pumping water into the potful of potatoes she had helped peel. She didn't want to know one word of the awful things Mama could imagine.

A day or so later, Pa came in at the end of his work and put a newspaper down on the table.

"Look at this," he said. Together Mama, Silas, and Kitty moved to the table to see, driven by something in Pa's voice.

"What's that? The *New York Times*?" Mama read in surprise. "Wherever did you get it?" They had only seen Pa's regular paper, the *Brattleboro Reformer*, before then.

"Given to me in town," Pa said, shaking his head. "Shows you how this whole thing is blowin' up. Won't hear the end of it now, even up here on our place. What are things comin' to?"

Kitty leaned forward to see where Pa's finger had pointed on the page. "'May 10, *New York Times*,'" she read aloud slowly. "'Accused by Rudyard Kipling, Beatty S. Balestier was brought before Justice Newton today, charged by his brother-in-law, Rudyard Kipling, with assault, opp . . . opp . . .

rob . . . ious language and attempt to kill. He was placed under . . .'" Here Kitty broke off. The letters seemed to jumble together on the page.

"Gosh," Silas said. "The *New York Times*!"

"The whole world will know now," Mama said, impressed.

"Oh, gosh," Silas said again. "Vermont's going to be famous! Dummerston's going to be famous! I can hardly wait!"

Pa looked sourly at him. "For what? It'll be *trouble*, more like, that you can't wait for," he said irritably. "And we don't go meetin' trouble halfway. You'd do well to remember that."

"Yes, Pa," Silas said, meeker now.

"What is oppro . . . oppro . . . language?" Kitty asked, hoping not to irritate Pa any further.

"Don't know," Pa replied. "But it sounds to me like language folks oughtn't to be using to each other."

The same thing was in all the local papers as well as in the *New York Times*. Some townspeople made fun of Mr. Kipling for getting worked up over nothing. Why, everybody knew Beatty Balestier would never kill a soul, didn't they?

⎯⎯⟨◇⟩⎯⎯

Over the next few days Kitty and Pa, watching from their porch, saw carriages full of reporters come streaming along the road toward or away from Naulakha.

"Where'd they all come from so sudden?" Kitty asked, astonished.

"From everywhere," Pa said glumly. "Boston, Philadelphia, New York, Washington. In for the kill, I reckon. Remember those two I picked up a couple of years ago? Said they'd get back at him? Well, now's their chance. Poor feller."

Pa sounded truly sorry for Mr. Kipling, even if he did resent the changes Mr. Kipling had brought into their lives.

Kitty nodded, staring out at the road. "I remember," she said.

At the very next moment another carriage came rumbling by. Seeing it, Pa and Kitty were so surprised, they both got to their feet. In it were several city-dressed reporters. And driving them along with a grin on his face was Beatty, no doubt taking them on a tour of Naulakha and other places of interest.

"Well, I'll be darned," Pa said. "I knew Beatty was out of jail on bond till the hearing, but that's not lookin' right to me."

Kitty sat down in her rocker with a bump. "I hope Mr. Kipling doesn't see him," she said.

"Ayuh," Pa agreed, shaking his head sorrowfully. "Well now, I don't guess Mr. Kipling ever expected this. Bet he thought Beatty would just get a good talkin' to from the sheriff, like a naughty schoolboy, and that'd be it. Maybe how they do it over in England or somethin'."

Kitty nodded again. Yes, that's what Mr. Kipling would have thought. That Beatty would be told what was the right way to behave and he would obey, like Mowgli and the wolf pack with the Law of the Jungle.

But it wasn't to be just a "talkin' to." It was to be a proper court hearing in front of the judge and in front of the whole wide world.

Rapidly, the town of Brattleboro filled up with spectators. Dozens of newspaper reporters hungrily reported every word of the famous writer's scandal.

And Kitty was miserable. Poor Mr. Kipling, she thought. She knew such an invasion of his privacy was the very thing he dreaded most, and she knew what it would mean to him. In the nights before the court hearing she lay awake almost until dawn. Her thoughts were at Naulakha, from where silence and shadows seemed to reach up to her through the dark woods.

The morning of the court hearing Mama watched as Kitty sat at the breakfast table without eating.

"Come now, Mary Sadie, eat up your porridge," she said. "You'll be falling asleep in school if you don't."

Kitty didn't move. "I can't, Mama," she said. "I just can't."

Silas dug heartily into his porridge. "I bet it's going to be a real show in town today," he said between mouthfuls.

Mama gave his arm a sharp pinch and sat down next to Kitty.

"Don't take it so hard," she said gently to Kitty. "I know how bad you feel for Mr. Kipling, but we can't change anything, can we? What will happen will happen."

"Well, I know what's going to happen!" Silas said. "They're going to send Beatty to jail, that's what! And it's not fair! Everybody's sayin' so."

Suddenly, Kitty turned and glared at him. "'Everybody's sayin' so,'" she mimicked. "Well, that's just the trouble. Everybody sayin' this and watchin' that." She got to her feet and stomped over to the window where outside, in pale sunshine, apple blossoms bounced up and down on a morning breeze. "Well, everybody should just leave Mr. Kipling alone. He's feeling bad enough already. He'd feel terrible if Beatty went to jail. He *likes* Beatty!"

"Of course he does," Mama said. "I'm sure he doesn't want that to happen."

"But nobody else will think that," Kitty exclaimed. "They'll blame it all on him."

Silas laughed. "Well, they won't think he's so great and important anymore, that's for sure," he said in a satisfied voice.

Kitty stamped her foot. "He doesn't want to be

great and important," she snapped. "He wants to be left alone. Why can't they just leave him be?"

She could see Silas and Mama looking at her in surprise. She could tell they would never understand. They would never know how much Mr. Kipling would hate to look foolish in the eyes of the townspeople, how he would hate to be laughed at. Well, she knew. And she wished with all her heart there was something she could do to help him.

"I'm going ahead of you," Kitty said abruptly to Silas, picking up the tin lunch pail Mama had prepared for her. Silas shrugged and waved his spoon at her. Mama got up and hugged her for a moment. Without another word Kitty put on her shawl and slipped out the door.

Walking quickly away from the house, she surprised two robins hopping in the fresh grass. Along the road, yellow daffodils poked their heads through last year's leaves, but Kitty barely saw them. Her heart was beating fast, faster than her steps, keeping time with what she was saying to herself; "Naulakha, Naulakha, I'm-going-to-Naulakha, Naulakha, Naulakha, I'm-going-to-Naulakha."

And she was. She must have decided it without even knowing it. What could she do to help Mr. Kipling? She would go to Naulakha and see. As simple as that.

It was cold, even in the sun where Kitty crouched behind one of the bushes Mr. Kipling had planted outside Naulakha. Pulling her shawl closer around her, she watched the Kiplings' carriage pull out of the driveway onto the road. She listened as its sound faded away down the hill. Above her she could hear Josephine's voice coming from the nursery window and a cry or two from Baby Elsie. The little girls were evidently staying home with Nanny while Mr. and Mrs. Kipling drove into Brattleboro for the court hearing.

After a while Kitty saw the door of the nursery open on the veranda above. "It's not cold, Nanny! It's not!" Josephine's voice said. "I don't want to wear my coat!"

Kitty jumped up and stood out in the open. "Josephine!" she called. "Hello!"

Josephine came to the veranda railing. She was

not tall enough to look over, but Kitty could just see her hand on the top edge.

"It's me—Kitty!" she called. "Go and ask Nanny if I can play with you today."

A brief silence, and then Josephine called, "Nanny! Kitty's here! Kitty's here!" Nanny, in her apron and her white cap, came and looked down at Kitty.

"Off to school, are you?" Nanny said. She looked quite pale and tired.

Kitty took a deep breath. "There isn't any today," she lied boldly. "Can I come in and play with Josephine?"

Nanny hesitated, then nodded, pointing down toward the front door, and Kitty went around the corner of the house to be let in.

Inside it was as gloomy as she had imagined. Naulakha's printed cotton curtains were pulled across its views; its rooms were silent and shadowed. Upstairs, Josephine made Kitty sit on the nursery floor, saying excitedly, "Now we can have a tea party!"

Nanny, finished folding laundry next to Elsie's cradle, came and sat down in a chair near Kitty.

"It's kind of you to come and play, Kitty," she said as Josephine trotted around happily with her teacups. "It will cheer us up no end, you know."

In a low voice, Kitty said, "I just saw the carriage leave for town. Is he . . . I mean, are Mr. and Mrs. Kipling awful upset, Nanny? What's going to happen, do you think? Do you know, Nanny?"

Nanny closed her eyes. "My dear child," she said, almost in a whisper. "That is a question I really cannot answer. Anything could happen. They are, as you say, 'awful upset.' The little ones feel it too." She nodded toward Josephine. "She misses the games and the stories quite dreadfully."

Later on, after they had had lunch, Kitty eating the cold potatoes and biscuits Mama had put in her lunch pail, they played outside for a while in the little wigwam Mr. Kipling had made for Josephine. On their way back to the house they saw the carriage returning and watched Matt Howard help Mr. and Mrs. Kipling climb out slowly. Josephine ran ahead and threw herself into their arms, chattering away. As Mr. Kipling

hugged her, he turned his gray and weary face and caught sight of Kitty.

"I can tell we have a happier little girl today," he said with a small smile. "I am very grateful to you, Kitty."

Kitty felt herself blush. Then, without thinking further, she blurted out, "I can come again! I can come tomorrow if you want me to! And every day! I mean, after school, I can come!"

"Can you?" Mr. Kipling said. "I should think Josephine would enjoy that very much. If it's all right with you, Nanny?"

"She would be most welcome, sir," Nanny said at once.

Mr. Kipling took Mrs. Kipling's arm. "And will that be agreeable, my dear?" he asked her.

Mrs. Kipling nodded, and even smiled briefly at Kitty. Then as they went slowly into the house, Mr. Kipling looked back at Nanny and the children. "Thank you, Kitty," he said.

Mama was stony-faced when Kitty got home.

"Pray tell," she said, "where have you been today, Mary Sadie?"

Behind Mama, Kitty could see Silas bent studiously over his schoolbooks. She had hoped she would meet up with him before he reached home to tell on her, but she had missed him on the way. Now there was nothing to be done but look Mama straight in the eye and say, "I'm very sorry, Mama. I was at Naulakha. I wanted to help, if I could."

Mama looked steadily back at her. "And did you help?"

Kitty nodded. "Yes, I did. I played with Josephine. Nanny said it was a good idea, and Mr. Kipling himself asked if I could come back."

"What?" Silas exclaimed. "And skip school again?"

"After school," Kitty explained calmly. "Every day. They really need someone to come and cheer Josephine up, Mama. You should see how gloomy it is there."

Mama listened to her in silence. Then to Kitty's surprise she said, "Yes, I'm sure this is a hard time for them. All right then. You may go *after* school for an hour or two. But I think it would be wise not to tell your Pa just yet. You hear me, Silas?"

Kitty breathed a sigh of relief. "Thank you, Mama," she said.

And with a frown Silas said, "Yes, Mama. I hear you."

"He was nervous?" Kitty asked Pa in a worried voice. "Please, Pa, was he very very nervous or just a little bit nervous?"

Pa had just come home with news of the court hearing even though he had not attended it. There had been far too many people crowding into the balconies in the town hall where it was held. "Like they were going to a state fair," he said scornfully. Later in the Brooks House Hotel he had asked several townspeople for news.

But before answering Kitty, Pa looked at her sternly. "Now see here, Miss Kitty," he said. "I'm telling you about this because I know it's somethin' important to you. But you know it's not your business, so don't go gettin' all upset about it. Like I always say, if your head is wax, don't go walkin' in the sun."

"No, Pa," Kitty mumbled.

"It's just *some* folks who say he was nervous," Pa

continued. "Crumplin' up his hat over and over, droppin' it on the floor and such. But some say he was mighty quick in answerin' the lawyer's questions. Had a good deal of fight in him."

"Did he?" Mama asked. "Like when, for instance?"

"Well," Pa said, trying to remember what he had been told, "seems they asked him about his comin' to Vermont to look after Beatty like he had promised the other brother, and was that what he spends his time doin' over here? And he said he might sometimes do a little writing as well. Somethin' like that anyway." Here Pa smiled slightly, knowing, as did everyone, what a great deal of writing Mr. Kipling really did.

"Tell you one thing," Pa went on. "Seems Mr. Kipling claimed he didn't think he had ever said to anyone he was payin' Beatty's way. Only that he had helped him out when he needed it. Said Beatty didn't owe him money at all right now, had paid back every penny."

Mama looked puzzled. "Then this whole thing is for nothing?" she asked.

"You mean there aren't any lies about Beatty for

Mr. Kipling to take back?" Kitty asked, astonished. "About holding him up by his britches, and all that?"

Pa rubbed his nose and sighed. "Well, o'course Beatty only knew what someone else told him. Didn't hear it himself. Problem is, he does admit threatenin' Mr. Kipling. Didn't have killin' him in mind, but to give him a mighty good beatin', or so he said."

"Well, they can't put him in jail for that!" Silas piped up.

Mama still looked puzzled. "Then it's all over?" she asked.

Kitty held her breath.

"Nope," Pa said. " Not by a long shot. There's got to be a trial anyway, because Mr. Kipling filed the complaint with the sheriff that Beatty threatened to kill him. Goin' for trial in September."

"Oh no!" Kitty wailed. "You mean there's going to be more?"

"Lots more," Pa said quietly.

"Is my daddy coming too?" That was Josephine, calling down the stairs at Naulakha as Kitty started up them. Each afternoon when Kitty went to play with her, Josephine asked the same question. But Mr. Kipling was not coming. He spent most of every day sleeping, too upset to do anything else. They almost never saw him at all.

Kitty tried hard to be cheerful for Josephine's sake. It wasn't easy; she missed Mr. Kipling too. They both missed the sound of his voice, his stories, and the funny things he said. And Kitty missed his kind answers to her many questions and the questions he asked her in turn.

But the questions were bigger now. What could the answer be to what would happen next? And to whether she was any help at all at Naulakha? There was no answer to the first. As for the second, well, she was doing the only thing she could.

"Let's play school," she said to Josephine. "We can take the dolls out on the porch. Then later we can go out and look for your wheelbarrow." Josephine had left her little wooden wheelbarrow outside the day before. Now she scampered off cheerfully to find her dolls.

A little later, when the dolls had learned their

ABCs from one of Josephine's books, a deep voice was heard inside the nursery saying, "Good afternoon, Nanny." And Mr. Kipling came out to them on the veranda and sat down stiffly in a rocking chair.

"Good afternoon, Madame Teacher, Miss Kipling, and others," he said. "I see I'm late for school. Please accept my apologies."

But in spite of his joking words, his voice was not as Kitty remembered it. It was slow and weary sounding, matching the way he looked.

"Daddy!" Josephine cried, rushing to climb onto his lap. Mr. Kipling hugged her closely. For a while nobody spoke. Below them a chipmunk went *chip-chip-chip* as it ran along a stone wall.

Josephine sat up. "You know what, Daddy? Yesterday I lost my wheelbarrow. But now you can come and help me find it."

Mr. Kipling turned so he could see the hill below them where it sloped away toward the road and Beatty's house. He shook his head. "Well, perhaps not right away," he said. "Maybe later when Matt Howard comes back from town. He's very good at finding wheelbarrows, you know."

Kitty heard his words, but clear as day she heard something else. With a new kind of listening she heard fear in his voice: Mr. Kipling's fear of meeting Beatty alone out there on the hillside he had come to love so much.

A few afternoons later, as she was leaving Naulakha, Kitty noticed Mr. Kipling putting papers and notebooks into a leather case. She could see him through the open door of his study as she was passing. He wasn't packing, was he?

"You're not going away, are you, Mr. Kipling?" she asked anxiously. "I mean for good or anything?"

How could he be when nothing else in the house was being packed, as far as she could see?

"No, well, just for a few days," Mr. Kipling said. "Dr. Conland and I are going to Boston again to have a look at coal schooners and such."

"Oh," Kitty said in relief. "For your book."

Mr. Kipling nodded. "Yes, it's time to get on with things." He gave his spectacles a few taps and looked around him vaguely. "And it might help all this to pass, don't you know?"

"Yes," Kitty said, without sounding very sure. "Well, I hope you have a real nice time. I'm just going home now, so good-bye, Mr. Kipling."

Kitty turned to leave, but Mr. Kipling came to the door of his study.

"I say, Kitty. You will still be able to come while I'm away, won't you?"

"Oh yes," Kitty said quickly. "I can come."

"I'm glad," Mr. Kipling said, giving her a half smile. "And perhaps, when I return, you can tell me how each day went in the nursery. You might even write a few things down to remember them by, if you like. Perhaps in a small notebook, how would that be?" Going to his desk he fetched a little notebook and handed it to her. "Could you use this, do you think?"

Kitty hesitated. "I'll try," she said, but without much confidence.

Mr. Kipling caught something in her tone. "This has all been very upsetting, I know, Kitty," he said. "I am so dreadfully sorry you had to be witness to it."

Kitty was silent, her eyes on the notebook in her hand.

"And your people," Mr. Kipling went on. "They are surely sorry for it as well. I think your father has always felt things changed greatly up here after I came. And not for the better, I might add. Have you felt that way too?"

Kitty shook her head vigorously, her eyes almost filling with tears. "Oh no, Mr. Kipling!" she declared. "If anything changed it was all for the *good,* not for the *bad,* really it was!"

"I hope so," Mr. Kipling said, looking hard at her. "And may I say," he added, "you are turning into a fine young American lady, Miss Kitty. To my mind, there is nothing better than that. Now run along."

Kitty ran.

Tears rolled down Kitty's cheeks as she went quickly along the shaded road home. Oh yes, things had changed. Even this road which she had known all her life. It might look the same, but every tree along it, every pebble under her feet, held new stories in it. The shapes of the trees and the colors of bushes and plants seemed somehow different. If they had once been understandable, boring and commonplace, now they seemed mysteriously to have become her companions. As if they had shared her experiences and become a part of what was happening, a part of her. Stopping in the road, Kitty looked up at the young leaves over her head—and somehow she felt she had never seen them before.

If Kitty's surroundings seemed different to her, so did the way time passed. It began to speed up like a runaway horse, with Kitty rattling around in a wagon behind it. Everything was happening very fast.

In only a few days, Mr. Kipling was back from Boston, a bit better in spirits. He even talked with enthusiasm of the smell of oilskins and decayed fish. He listened with interest to Kitty's accounts from her notebook and praised her for them. Then he was off again, this time to Canada.

As Kitty sat at her new writing table, her notebook soon filled up with tales of her afternoons at Naulakha, and sometimes with her own thoughts as well.

To Mr. Kipling, when he returned, she read her entries about Josephine:

"Josephine likes to tell me I'm wrong when I call things by their American names. 'It's not called candy, Kitty, it's sweets. Not lima beans, Kitty, broad beans! Not a jump rope, Kitty, it's a skipping rope! Nanny says so.' But she's just teasing me. She's mighty American herself by now."

or

"Josephine tells Baby Elsie the animal stories Mr. Kipling tells to her, about the elephant's trunk and the camel's hump. But sometimes she mixes them up and gives the elephant a hump and the camel a trunk. She's funny and we laugh."

But other entries she kept for herself.

"I like to watch Pa when he comes home at night. He always wipes his boots off before he comes in. He looks around to see that we, and

everything, are all right. Then he sits down and reads his paper."

or

"A bird flew against the kitchen window today. It fell in the grass and breathed up and down very fast. It flew away after a while. I think it thought the window was a tree because it reflects leaves in it just like in a mirror."

But one night she wrote in her notebook;

"When Mama and I were fixing supper, she said folks talk about Mr. Kipling's trips away from Vermont. They have heard he might go to England this year, and they think he won't be back in time for Beatty's trial. They say if that happens there won't even be a trial. I think about that too, but I don't ask about it. I just don't want to. But how does Mama always know what's in my mind?"

For Kitty, writing in her notebook helped slow things down. It caught and held them so she could think about them later.

One hot afternoon at Naulakha, she longed for her notebook so she could write in it exactly what Mr. Kipling had just said. It was time for her to go home, but they were still sitting out on the nursery veranda, Kitty, Josephine, and Mr. Kipling. The sky, completely empty of clouds, a perfect blue, stretched above Mt. Wantastiquet and Mt. Monadnock way across the valley. Katydids sang. Beyond the meadow below them a row of dark pines stood as still as soldiers. They seemed to Kitty to be holding their breath, just as she was doing, listening to Mr. Kipling as he said, "You may remember an idea I had, Kitty, before Elsie was born, to visit England this year?"

There it was, just what Mama had been talking about!

Kitty nodded, remembering very well Mr. Kipling's worries about the war. She knew it still worried him. Now Mr. Kipling paused and looked across the green hills to Mt. Monadnock, that "giant thumbnail pointing heavenward," as he called it.

"Well, I think we may be going off on that road, one of these days," he said. "Joining up again with the wind that tramps the world."

Kitty's heart sank down to her toes.

"Oh," she said in a small voice. "You mean for a long time?"

"Well, I don't know exactly," Mr. Kipling answered. He gave her a faint smile. "But you know I wouldn't want to miss the wood anemones when they bloom here in the spring, would I?"

Kitty did not return his smile. She had immediately understood something—that even if Mr. Kipling would not *want* to miss the anemones, he *would* miss them, and then he would miss Beatty's trial in September as well.

And in that very same instant, Kitty knew something else, something much more important. She knew an ending was coming. It was crystal clear to her, as if she were looking down into a quiet brook where she could see every single pebble along the bottom. She knew Mr. Kipling would be leaving, yes, but not just for some months; *she knew he would be leaving forever.* Josephine and Elsie would be leaving.

Mrs. Kipling and Nanny and Matt Howard would be leaving. There would be no more dolls' tea parties in the nursery. There would be no more games in the garden. Storytelling would be over. Snow-golf would be over. The only thing left would be memories and unanswered questions.

Facing these truths, Kitty sat without moving. Mr. Kipling watched her quietly. Then he said, "You know, if I ever did have to leave here, I should lose someplace where I felt I really belonged. I have searched for such a place since childhood. But," he added with a sigh, "I have always sensed the possibility of losing any delights life might bring." Here he paused and looked thoughtfully at Josephine as she played with her dolls.

Listening to Mr. Kipling, Kitty felt he was talking more to himself than to her.

"I should perhaps have been better at all this," he continued, but so softly that Kitty could barely hear him. "Better at following the rituals of this strange tribe. I write of Mowgli, of obedience to the pack and the law, of courage and of action. Well, the world will certainly laugh at this show of courage and action, won't it? Mowgli would have managed it much better, yes indeed."

Mr. Kipling lapsed into silence, which the katy-dids filled with their rhythmic singing. Then, after a bit he went on, saying, "And you know, my dear, this question of fame . . . it rather upsets the order of things, doesn't it? I thought no one could touch me up here in this precious jewel of mine. But it seems I was mistaken."

At the resigned tone of his voice, Josephine put down her dolls and came to climb up in his lap. He hugged her and then, suddenly, tickled her in the ribs, making her giggle helplessly.

"Now wouldn't it be difficult, Miss Kipling," he said cheerily, "to leave a place where one has raised ones kids, and builded a wall,"—he took her hand and pointed it to one down in the garden—"and digged a well," he pointed her hand toward Naulakha's well—"and planted a tree"—here he directed her hand toward the many he had planted—"wouldn't it be difficult, wouldn't it?"

Then with a smile he set Josephine, still giggling, onto the veranda floor and got to his feet.

"Now I must think about dressing for dinner," he said, still cheerful, "and other disgusting things such as washing and hair brushing. But it has got to be did." Turning to look at Kitty he said, "And you, my dear, I have kept you far too long today. You must be on your way. Let's go and find Nanny, shall we?"

Silently, Kitty nodded, and, taking Josephine by the hand, she followed him into the nursery.

"Are you all right, Mary Sadie?" Mama asked a while later, as Kitty came up the porch steps. "You look mighty tired. Maybe you better come right home after school from now on. They can do without you at Naulakha."

"I'm all right, Mama," Kitty replied quickly. "I didn't sleep so well last night. There was a . . . a . . . cricket in my room."

"Better find it and put it out, then," Mama said. "Won't do to miss your sleep and fall sick."

"No, Mama," Kitty said. She sat down on the top step, below where Mama sat stringing beans. For a few moments there was silence.

Then Mama said, "I reckon they'll be leavin' soon, won't they?"

Kitty nodded without answering, smoothing the skirt of her dress tightly around her knees, over and over.

Mama stopped stringing beans. "Likely as not, they won't be back for Beatty's trial, will they?" she said. "So I s'pose Beatty'll go around actin' swell-headed for a while, but don't worry, he'll quiet down by the time they *do* come back. Things'll be all right, you'll see."

It was more than Kitty could bear. She began to cry, and Mama set down her bowl of beans and came and sat next to Kitty and put her arms around her and held her.

"Hush now," Mama said. "Hush now, honey. Everything's going to be all right in time."

"No it isn't," Kitty sobbed against Mama's apron. But Mama didn't hear, and Kitty knew that for once Mama didn't know what was in Kitty's mind, had no idea of what was really going to happen. Drawing a shaky breath, quieter now, Kitty decided to keep what she knew to herself. Who would take her word for it, anyway?

In August the Kiplings began to pack. They said they were going to England to visit the family. People accepted it; after all, they had done it before. And if Mr. Kipling did not come back in time for the September trial, it was his business. Perhaps everything would be forgotten by the time he returned. It was much better that way.

But for Kitty it was unbearable to be at Naulakha. Luckily Pa needed her for haying, and Mama needed her in the vegetable garden. But once in a while, if she had time, she was drawn there against her will, as if by a magnet.

On one of those days, she helped Josephine pack some of her dolls for the trip.

"You can leave the others over there in the rocker," Kitty suggested, trying to sound cheerful. "They'll be all right till . . . till you come back. You can give them a book to read, if you want." She could see that Josephine was excited about the trip. It would only confuse her to see Kitty with a gloomy face.

Another time she was there, she met Mr. Kipling in the hall as she was leaving.

"I'm sorry to always be so busy," he said to her. "Not much time for chatting, is there? Must decide what to take, what to leave here, and all that."

"I know," Kitty said. "And I'm not here very much. I'm helping with the haying."

Mr. Kipling nodded. "Of course you are. Haying time again. Wonderful to see the seasons come round. You know, Kitty," he said, suddenly more serious, "one of these days we'll be off, and if I shouldn't see you before that, I think . . . yes, I think I'd like to say good-bye now."

Kitty froze. It had come. Just like that. The ending had come. Already. All at once. Suddenly. Now. Not as she had pictured it, no. But how had she pictured it? She had no idea. She hardly heard Mr. Kipling speak again.

"You will remember I promised to give you a special copy of *The Jungle Book,* won't you?" he said. "I want you to have one from England, a first edition. I'll send it to you as soon as we arrive. In the meantime, I'm going to give you a few more of my notebooks to write your observations in. You must go on observing, Kitty. You already see a lot of things others don't. And you'll be seeing more. *Everything* is worth observing. Will you remember that?"

"Yes," Kitty said, willing herself not to cry. Mr. Kipling went into his study and brought out several notebooks. He put them in her hands.

"Good-byes are not easy," he said gruffly.

Kitty swallowed hard. Not looking at him, she said, "Pa tells us short good-byes and long hellos are best."

Mr. Kipling smiled. "He's a very wise man," he said. And then Mr. Kipling put his arms around Kitty and gave her a gentle hug. "So we'll do just that. Good-bye, Kitty, my dear. Thank you for everything."

And Kitty, with her hands against his warm jacket, said, "Good-bye, Mr. Kipling. Thank you, too."

Somehow she managed to get out the door before bursting into tears.

How long had she been sitting there on the stone wall? Kitty couldn't tell. Her tears had dried and her snuffling had long stopped. But still she sat there, a

bit back from the road, just out of sight of Naulakha, in a leafy place from which she looked out over a meadow.

She sat there, thinking about nothing at all. Nothing. Next to her, on a flat stone, lay Mr. Kipling's notebooks. An ant crawled slowly across them and down over the edges of the rocks to the ground. Kitty watched it without interest. Then another ant followed. And behind that two more. Across the notebooks, down the edges of the rocks, to the leafy ground below. When, one by one, still more ants came after the first, they caught Kitty's eye. Slowly her mind awakened and asked itself where the ants might be going.

Bending down, Kitty pushed leaves and grass aside with her hands. The ant trail led under a stone fallen there from the wall. Crouching down, Kitty watched them: ordinary ants going under an ordinary stone. Then, without thinking, she turned the stone over.

"Oh!" she said out loud, surprising herself, for after all, she had often turned stones over and seen bugs and creatures scurry away to hide. The acorn weevils and the centipede she saw now were familiar to her. So were the beetle grub and the wiggling tip of an earthworm. And there, where across the leaves tiny red spider mites crawled, was the ant trail, leading down into a hole in the earth.

But now, fascinated, Kitty crouched there watching until her knees ached. When at last she stood up, she looked around her slowly, with wide eyes. Then, putting the stone back where it had been, she started for home.

This time she walked in the meadow, following the stone wall, instead of taking the road.

She was thinking of how that night she would write in her notebook what she had just seen: ordinary things, but somehow not so ordinary after all.

And then she stopped where she was and bent down again. Parting the stems of tall grasses by the wall, Kitty closed her hand around something lying there.

Straightening up, she opened her hand and looked at what it held. It was just as she had thought. Though its pink color had faded, and wet earth had stained it, Kitty had immediately known what it was when she glimpsed it in the grass. It was a lost golf ball from Mr. Kipling's games of snow-golf.

Holding it carefully, as if it were a delicate bird's egg, Kitty smiled, and then, almost running, she turned up the hill toward home.

Afterword

Rudyard Kipling's four years in Vermont were surely his happiest. His later life, filled as it was with great acclaim, including the Nobel Prize for Literature in 1907, was also filled with widespread disapproval due to his perceived imperialist views, as well as with personal tragedy.

In 1899, only three years after leaving Vermont, he lost his beloved daughter Josephine. Both Kipling and Josephine had fallen seriously ill during a family trip from England to New York to see his publishers. Kipling just barely survived, but little Josephine, aged six, did not.

Throughout the rest of his life, Kipling was haunted not only by Josephine's death, but also by the death of his son, John, who in 1917, at the age of eighteen, was killed in the First World War. But Kipling always remembered his years in Vermont with heartfelt pleasure, frequent longing, and many regrets.

Rudyard Kipling died in London in 1936, after a lifetime of world fame and considerable wealth. He is remembered everywhere for his vast amount of writings: articles, verses, short stories, novels, and, above all, for *The Jungle Book,* as well as the *Just So Stories,* many of which he had made up and told to Josephine while in Vermont.

Kipling's political views were, and still are, controversial. He was considered, and still is considered by many to have been, an imperialist, a racist, and a militarist. But imperialism, racism, and militarism were widely held views at that time, and recently opinions about him have softened somewhat. In his personal life he always had a great affinity for children.

Rudyard Kipling's ashes are buried in Poets' Corner in Westminster Abbey, in London.

In writing of Kipling's time in Vermont, I have followed the facts as closely as possible, drawing on the many biographies written about him. Some of the spoken words I have given him in this book contain actual expressions he used, taken from his letters and articles. The rest I have made up.

Kitty, and her friendship with Mr. Kipling, I have wholly invented. His part in the story is really just a background to the main story, which is rightfully Kitty's.

Naulakha, like a forest-green ship, with its verandas and its loggia, can still be seen in Vermont. It still faces Mr. Kipling's favorite view over valley and hill, out to Mt. Monadnock, that "giant thumbnail pointing heavenward." Farther along the road, which is still just bumpy dirt, Beatty's house, Maplewood, still stands. A bit farther along, on a stretch of hilly farmland, is where Kitty herself might well have lived.

Bibliography

Books

Amis, Kingsley. *Rudyard Kipling*. New York: Thames and Hudson, 1986.

Carrington, Charles. *Rudyard Kipling: His Life and Work*, rev. ed. London: Macmillan and Co., 1978.

Dobree, Bonamy. *Rudyard Kipling: Realist and Fabulist*. London: Oxford University Press, 1967.

Franklin, Benjamin. *Poor Richard's Almanack*. Mount Vernon, New York: Peter Pauper Press, 1983.

Kipling, Rudyard. *From Sea to Sea and Other*

Sketches: Letters of Travel. London: Macmillan and Co., 1912.

Kipling, Rudyard. *The Jungle Books*. 1894 and 1895. Reprint, London: Penguin Books, 1994.

Kipling, Rudyard. *Just So Stories*. 1902. Reprint, Hertfordshire: Wordsworth Editions, 1993.

Kipling, Rudyard. *O Beloved Kids: Rudyard Kipling's Letters to His Children*. London: Arrow Books, 1984.

Kipling, Rudyard. *Something of Myself: For My Friends Known and Unknown*. 1937. Reprint, London: Penguin Books, 1992.

Laski, Marghanita. *From Palm to Pine: Rudyard Kipling Abroad and at Home*. London: Sidgwick and Jackson, 1987.

Lycett, Andrew. *Rudyard Kipling*. London: Weidenfeld and Nicolson, 1999.

Murray, Stuart. *Rudyard Kipling in Vermont: Birthplace of the Jungle Books*. Bennington, Vermont: Images from the Past, 1997.

Nicolson, Adam. *The Hated Wife: Carrie Kipling 1862–1939*. London: Short Books, 2001.

Pitkin, Olive. *There and Then: A Vermont Childhood*. Santa Barbara, California: Fithian Press, 1997.

Rice, Howard C. *Rudyard Kipling in New England*. Rev. ed. Brattleboro, Vermont: The Book Cellar, 1951.

Ricketts, Harry. *The Unforgiving Minute: A Life of Rudyard Kipling*. London: Chatto and Windus, 1999.

Seymour-Smith, Martin. *Rudyard Kipling*. London: Queen Anne Press, 1989.

Taylor, Helen V. *A Time to Recall: The Delights of a Maine Childhood.* New York: W. W. Norton, 1963.

Van de Water, Frederic F. *Rudyard Kipling's Vermont Feud.* 1935. Reprint, Rutland, Vermont: Academy Books, 1981.

Articles

Day, Reverend C. O., "Rudyard Kipling as Seen in his Vermont Home." *The Congregationalist* (Vermont), March 16, 1899.

Huguenin, Charles A., "Rudyard Kipling and Brattleboro." *Vermont History,* vol. 24, no. 1 (1956).

Potter, H. D., "Rudyard Kipling and the First World War." *Kipling Journal,* vol. 74, no. 296 (2000).

Wallace, John A., "A Tale of Bliss and Tragedy." Exhibition Catalog (1994), Brattleboro Museum and Art Center.

The New York Times, 10 May 1896.

Grateful thanks to:

Brooks Memorial Library, Brattleboro, Vermont, for allowing me access to assorted Kipling files; to Mary White of Marlboro College Library, Marlboro, Vermont, for allowing me access to Kipling files there; to Carol Barber of The Landmark Trust, USA, for permission to visit Naulakha; and to A P Watt Ltd. on behalf of the National Trust for Places of Historical Interest or Natural Beauty for permission to quote from *The Jungle Book* by Rudyard Kipling.